Hoover Dam

Lori Dittmer

Creative Education • Creative Paperbacks

Road map of

Contents

Hoover Dam

border of Nevada and Arizona

Welcome to Hoover Dam! It blocks the Colorado River in the southwestern United States. Nevada is on the west side. Arizona is on the east.

Hoover Dam is an arch-gravity dam. It is thicker at the bottom than at the top. Standing 726 feet (221 m) tall, it is one of the largest concrete structures in the country!

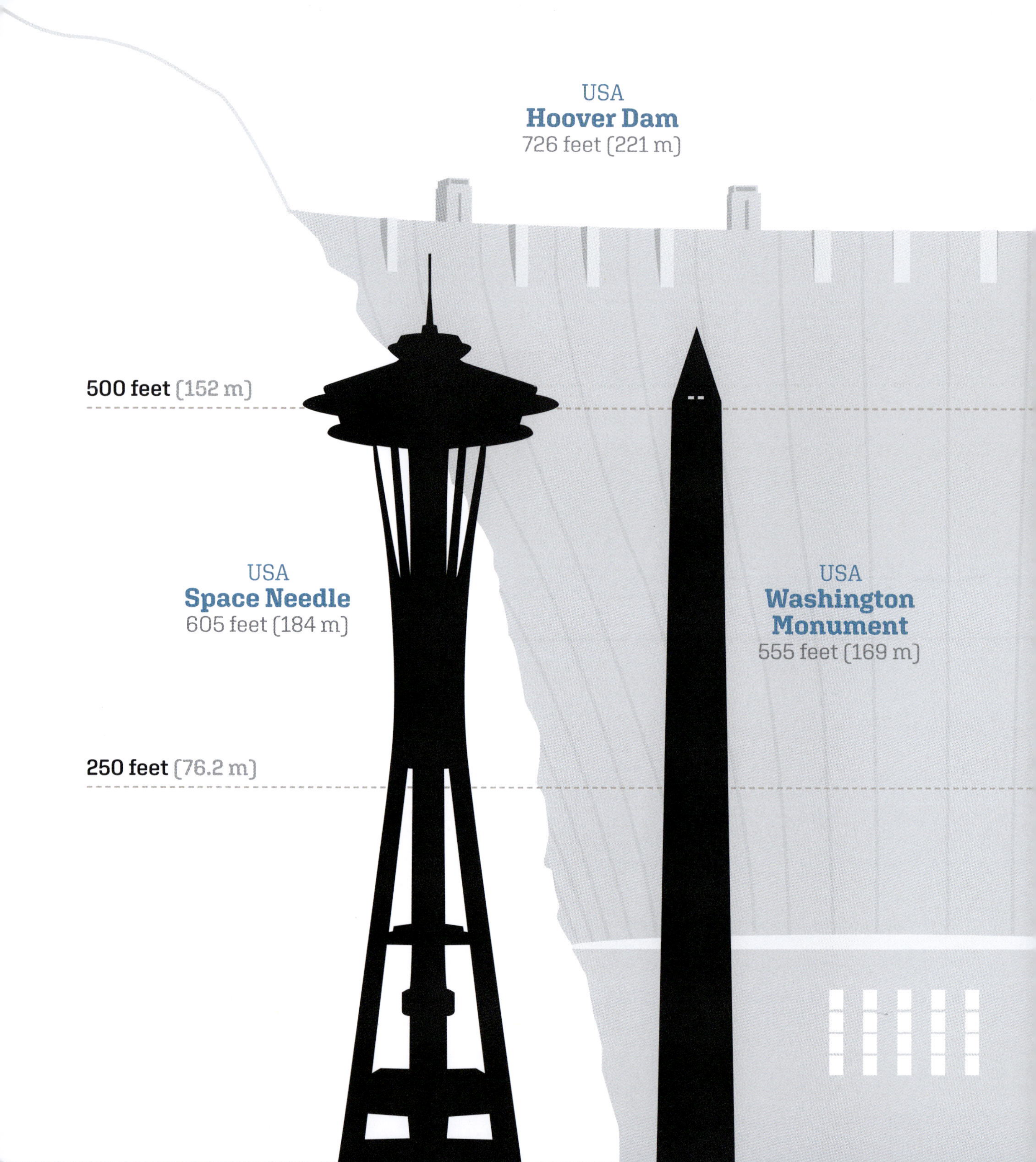
USA
Hoover Dam
726 feet (221 m)
500 feet (152 m)
250 feet (76.2 m)
USA
Space Needle
605 feet (184 m)
USA
Washington Monument
555 feet (169 m)

How tall is the Hoover Dam?

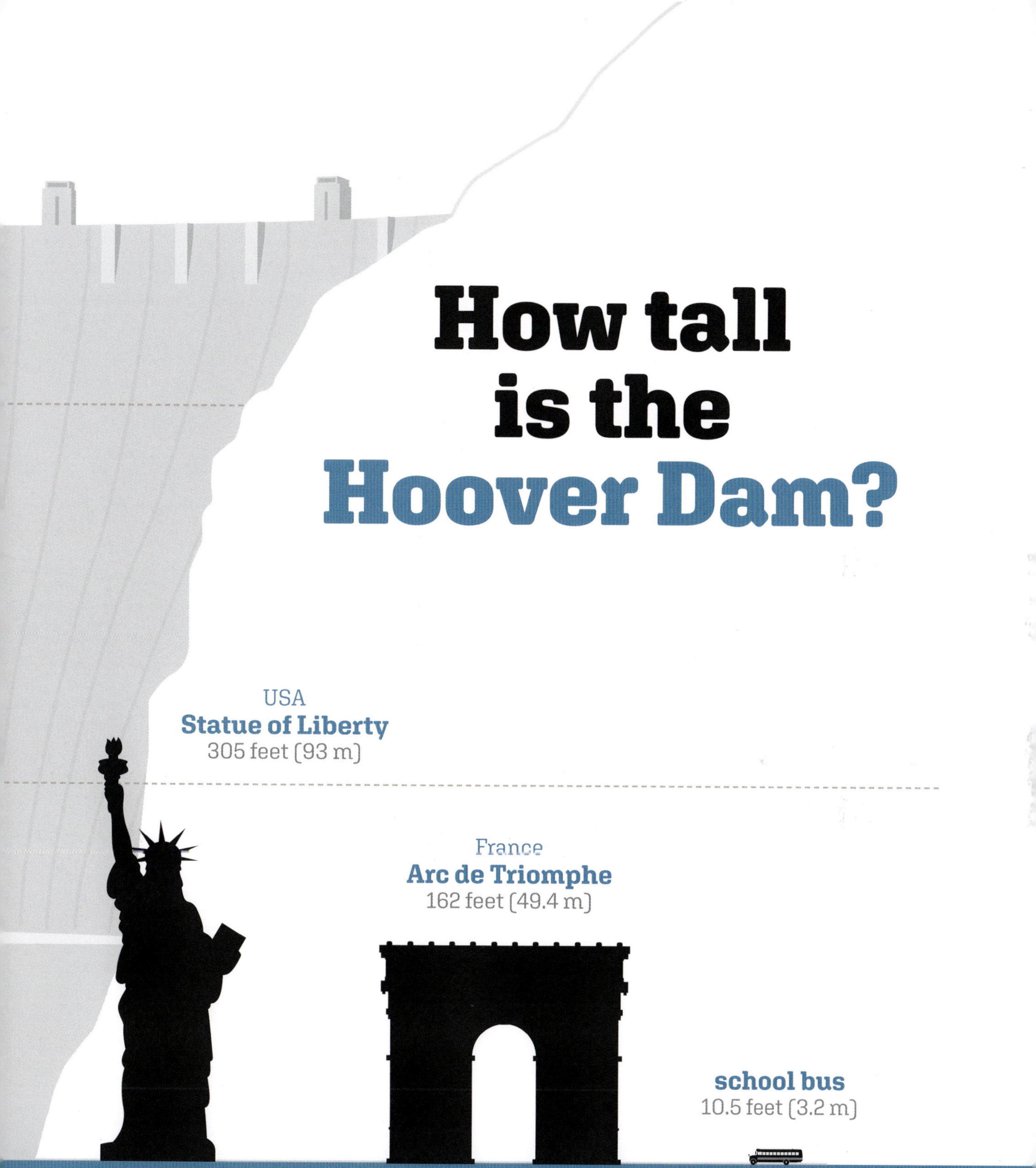

The Colorado River used to flood nearby farms and communities. The U.S. government decided to build a dam to control the river.

Planners wanted to build the dam in Boulder Canyon. Later, they chose Black Canyon for its stronger rock walls. But they still called it Boulder Dam. In 1947, it became Hoover Dam. Former U.S. president Herbert Hoover had helped with its early plans.

Herbert Hoover ►

In 1931, builders blasted tunnels through the canyon. This made the river run around the construction site. **High scalers** took loose rock from canyon walls. Other workers poured more than 5 million barrels of concrete. The dam is 660 feet (201 m) thick at the base. It is 45 feet (13.7 m) thick at the top.

◄ High scalers working on Hoover Dam

The dam opened in 1936. Its **reservoir** is named Lake Mead. Farms and homes get water from the lake. A power plant at the dam makes **hydroelectricity** for the area, too.

Can you spot these in the big picture?

Mike O'Callaghan–Pat Tillman Memorial Bridge

intake tower

Lake Mead

More than 7 million people visit Hoover Dam each year. You can walk or drive across the dam. South of the dam, a bridge crosses the river. Walk across for another view of the dam.

Many people visit nearby Lake Mead Recreation Area. Find a fishing spot, go for a boat ride, or hike along the lake.

20 ADULT LIFE JACKETS

★ Activity ★

Build a Dam

materials

popsicle sticks

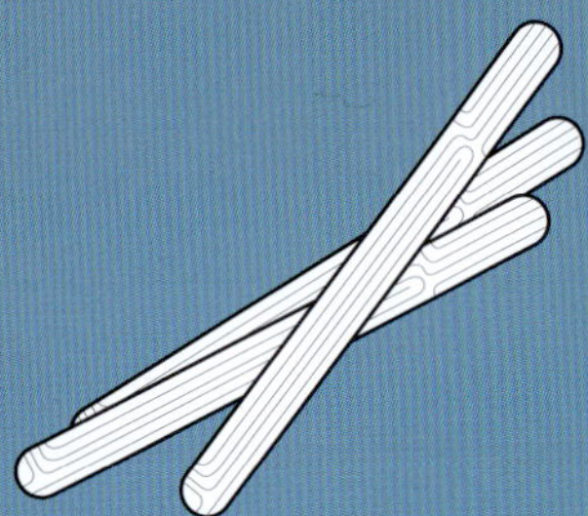

plastic container

long and shallow

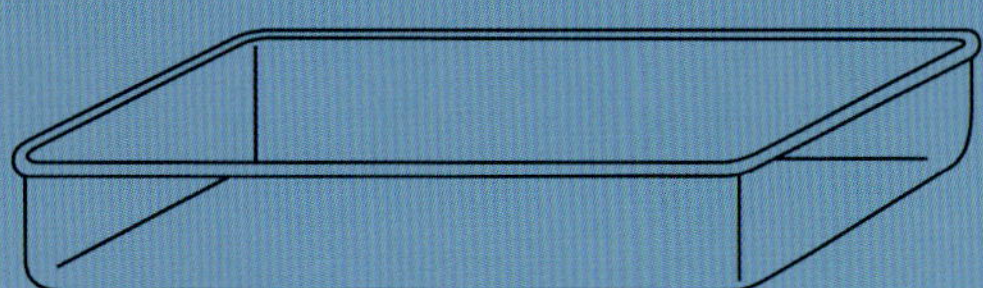

sand

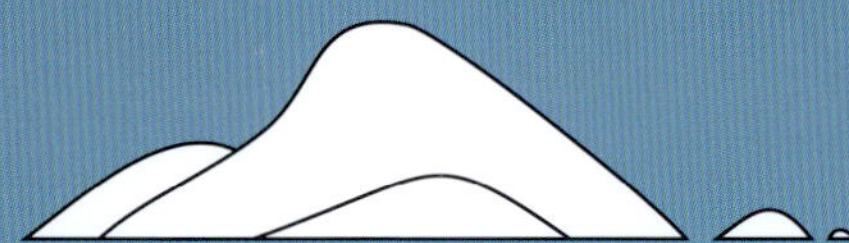

small rocks

(like aquarium gravel)

water

1

Fill the container with sand.

2

Make a path in the sand for the river.

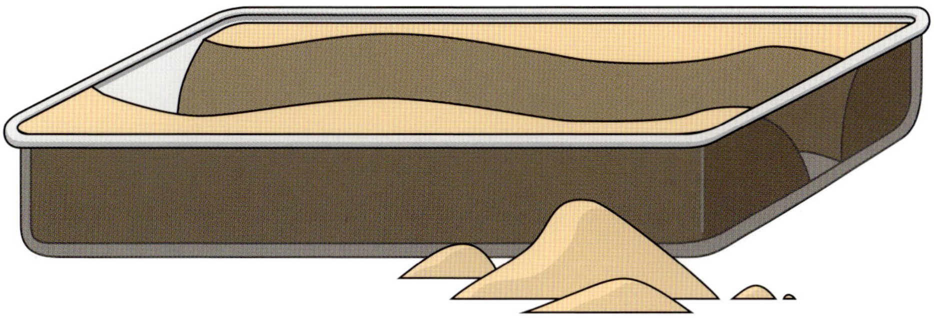

3

Pick a spot to block the river. Use popsicle sticks and rocks to build a dam.

4

Pour water into the river's path. Did your dam stop the water?

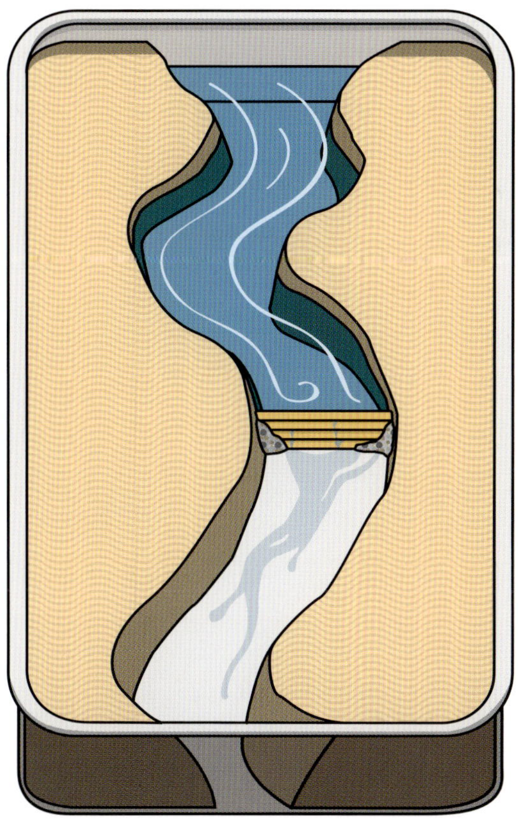

Glossary

high scalers
construction workers who climbed down canyon walls on ropes to remove loose rocks

hydroelectricity
electricity produced by flowing water

reservoir
a large lake where water is stored for use

Read More

Graham, Ian. *You Wouldn't Want to Work on the Hoover Dam!: An Explosive Job You'd Rather Not Do*. New York: Franklin Watts, 2012.

Stefoff, Rebecca. *Building the Hoover Dam*. New York: Cavendish Square, 2018.

Websites

PBS: Building Big: The Dam Challenge
Play this game to figure out what to do when dams have problems.

http://www.pbs.org/wgbh/buildingbig/dam/challenge/

YouTube: Building the Hoover Dam
Watch a video about the history and construction of the Hoover Dam.

https://www.youtube.com/watch?v=n9Gy_1Ppw5U

Index

PUBLISHED BY CREATIVE EDUCATION AND CREATIVE PAPERBACKS
P.O. Box 227, Mankato, Minnesota 56002
Creative Education and Creative Paperbacks are imprints of The Creative Company
www.thecreativecompany.us

LIBRARY OF CONGRESS CATALOGING-IN-PUBLICATION DATA
Names: Dittmer, Lori, author.
Title: Hoover Dam / Lori Dittmer.
Series: Landmarks of America.
Includes bibliographical references and index.
Summary: Examining the building process from the ground up, this high-interest title covers the history and construction of the Hoover Dam, one of Nevada and Arizona's most well-known landmarks.

Identifiers: LCCN: 2018061067
ISBN 978-1-64026-126-6 (hardcover)
ISBN 978-1-62832-689-5 (pbk)
ISBN 978-1-64000-244-9 (eBook)

Subjects: LCSH: Hoover Dam (Ariz. and Nev.)—Juvenile literature. / Dams—Design and construction—Juvenile literature. / Water-supply—Southwest, New—Juvenile literature.
Classification: LCC TC557.5.H6 D58 2019
DDC 627/.820979313—dc23

DESIGN AND PRODUCTION
by Joe Kahnke; art direction by Rita Marshall
Printed in China

PHOTOGRAPHS by Alamy (David Kilpatrick, Erik Lattwein, Lebrecht Music & Arts, Ron Niebrugge), Getty Images (Christina Felschen/Moment, James Forte/National Geographic Image Collection, PhotoQuest/Archive Photos, Derek E. Rothchild/The Image Bank, University of Southern California/Corbis Historical), iStockphoto (Pavliha), Shutterstock (Allard One, BATKA, dikobraziy, josep perianes jorba, Ranier Lesniewski, Piotr Przyluski, Alexey Pushkin, turtix)

FIRST EDITION HC 9 8 7 6 5 4 3 2 1
FIRST EDITION PBK 9 8 7 6 5 4 3 2 1